ANNABELLE

ANNABELLE

AN OWENS CHRONICLES NOVELLA

AMANDA LYNN PETRIN

CHAPTER 1

"I bet I could reach that branch," Embry said while we walked through the forest that surrounded my father's property. We had been over the bridge to play in the part of the creek where it wasn't so deep, so we could splash around a bit to cool off. I dreamed of being able to take off my boots and slip my feet into the icy waters, but I loved my father too much to give him a heart attack.

"I bet I could get as high as that one," Gabriel pointed to a slightly smaller branch a few feet higher than the first. Everything was a competition with those two. They were equally matched in the sense that they each dominated different fields; Gabriel would win any races, but Embry could take anyone in a wrestling match, and so on. Climbing was fair game, though it always made me nervous. Embry was stronger, so he could lift himself up easier, but Gabriel was lighter and could usually go higher if the tree was weaker at the top, such as this one.

"I can outclimb the both of you on that tree," I said, walking past them. They both stopped, looked at each other, then turned to me.

"How high do you think you can go?" Embry asked me skeptically.

"To the top," I said like it wasn't a big deal.

"Really?" Embry asked, sizing me up. "What are we betting?"

"Bragging rights," I smiled. My father had become more diligent about not letting me 'muck around like a child' lately, but I was sure I hadn't lost my old skills yet.

"Loser has to bring the toffee next week," Embry looked so smug that I understood why they were so obsessed with beating each other.

"Deal," I shook his hand.

"Gabriel?" Embry turned to his best friend when he didn't take the bet.

"I'm sitting this one out," Gabriel raised his hands in innocence and surrender.

"Afraid to lose to a girl?" Embry teased.

"More like I know that this particular girl can beat both of us when it comes to trees. My money is on her."

"She won't like you more if you suck up," Embry warned.

"This isn't me sucking up or flattering her ego. I know I can beat you at this, but I also know that she climbs to the top of Old Henderson's steeple and we barely make it halfway."

"Climbed," Embry corrected, looking at my attire, that was definitely more restrictive than it used to be. "Can you even climb in that dress?"

"I can climb in anything," I said defiantly in response to his doubt, rather than because of my confidence.

"Ladies first?" Embry turned to me. "Or no, you said you could outclimb me, that was the bet."

"You have to go first," Gabriel agreed.

"What do I get if I prove you wrong?" Embry asked him,

skipping the lowest branch and pulling himself up onto one that was taller than him.

"I'll do your chores tomorrow."

"For a week," Embry leveraged.

"For a month," Gabriel smiled to me.

"We'll leave it at the week," Embry shook his head as he rose higher and higher in the tree. I was more nervous watching him than I was of going up myself.

"Regretting your decision?" I asked Gabriel, mostly to distract myself from watching Embry climb branch after branch on a tree that didn't look capable of supporting him.

"Never. I would bet on you any day."

"Does that make you a fool?" I asked.

"It makes me someone who knows you don't make false claims. If you say you will do something, you will. You're honest to a fault."

"That's a lot of pressure," I couldn't help but smile at the way he was looking at me.

"You're good for it." He smiled and looked up to see Embry pass the point he said he would climb to, then reach the branch Gabriel had said he'd reach.

Embry looked down at us and asked, "Do you think you'll make it this high?"

"Wouldn't you like to know," I called up.

He smiled down at me, his blond hair catching in the wind, then went a little higher, but the branches at the top would not support his weight.

"Do I stay here so we can tell how high I got?" he asked.

"I would have the advantage of using you to climb higher."

"I guess I'll come down then." His smug smile lasted the entire time he climbed down, and only got bigger once he was standing tall at the bottom.

"Congratulations," I told him. "You beat your expectations."

"I did. And I'm okay with leaving it at that," he assured me with a smile that drove the other girls in town crazy. They were the reason my father kept pushing me to act more like a lady, so he could find a nice, strong, powerful, well-to-do man to marry me and take over the estate. I was lucky that my father wanted me to be happy, so he wanted someone who would also love and take care of me...hence the acting, and looking, more like a lady.

"Afraid you'll lose to a girl?" I threw his own words back at him.

"Would you like a boost?" he offered.

"I think that would be cheating," I ventured before lifting my skirts so I could use the lower branch as a step to reach the higher one Embry started with.

I moved slowly at first, but my muscles remembered as soon as I got going. I couldn't do it as effortlessly as Embry, but I had a sure foot and a strong grip.

"There's a nest up here!" I whispered excitedly when I was a few branches below Embry's original target.

"Robins, I think," he agreed.

"They're not just eggs, there's little babies!"

"We've been yelling since we got here, whispering now won't make a difference," Gabriel whispered up. I could tell from his voice that he was laughing at me.

"The chicks are sleeping. Now that I know, I have to be considerate of that," I pointed out, taking one last look before continuing on my way.

The trees grew thinner the higher I got, and from Gabriel's target I could see my home, where my parents would die if they saw me. I went slower from there, testing each branch before I put any weight on it.

"Congratulations, Monkey," Gabriel called up to me.

"You can climb," Embry was impressed.

"You knew that, Embry Dante. You just thought I got old and forgot."

"I thought it wasn't considered ladylike, but I stand corrected."

"Thank you," I pretended to tip my hat down to him, then tested the next branch.

"You can come down now Annabelle, you won," Gabriel pointed out.

"I won against Embry, but I said I could reach the top," I reminded them.

"We believe you," Gabriel called up.

There was some murmuring before Embry agreed, "We believe you can get to the tip of the tallest branch."

"Maybe I don't," I argued before going up a couple more branches. I paused near the top to feel the wind in my face, but it also made the branches sway, which I wasn't entirely comfortable with. There were three branches between me and what I considered the top. I was currently sitting to take in the view, and to make the branches stop moving.

"Come on, Belle!" Gabriel called up to me.

"I'll be down in a minute," I said, smiling to myself at how I said it as if I was simply coming down the stairs, rather than climbing down a tree.

"Do you enjoy causing heart attacks?" Gabriel pressed.

"What do you call cliff diving?"

"Fun," they said in unison.

"I call it a million ways to die of stupidity, so I say we're even."

"What are you even doing up there?" Embry asked, and I could hear the concern.

"You'll see," I was standing as tall as I could without using the top two branches, as they didn't feel secure. I took the long white ribbon from my curly brown hair and tied it around the highest branch I could reach. "Alright, catch me if I fall," I called out before making my way down.

"You better not…" Gabriel warned.

"You can't tell me what to do," I teased, careful not to get overly confident until I was on the ground.

"Can I ask you very politely to please not fall, because my heart would never recover if I didn't catch you, or if you got injured in any way."

"Same here," Embry voiced.

"It sounds to me like men have the weaker hearts."

"Definitely," Gabriel agreed.

"We can do the scary stuff, no problem but my heart… don't ask me to watch someone I love in danger or in pain."

"I would much rather be the one in pain," Gabriel said.

"Pathetic," I teased, passing the nest with the robins.

"You, Miss Owens, are unlike any other lady I've ever met," Gabriel gave me a hand once I got to the last branch.

"Possibly because I am not a lady."

"You are, according to your father."

"Yes, he wants me to grow up and be proper, but until summer is over…"

"You get to be a girl," Embry shrugged, causing me to raise an eyebrow at him. "Which is clearly a very good thing. Have I mentioned my best friend is a girl?"

"I thought I was your best friend?" Gabriel pretended to be offended.

"I have two," Embry assured him.

"Same," I smiled at them.

"Me three," Gabriel agreed.

"Come on, let's get you home before your father sees the state of you," Embry put an end to the moment.

"I'm more afraid of her mother," Gabriel warned.

My father was stern when needed, but I was his beloved little girl who could do no wrong, whose happiness was his main concern. My mother's job was turning me into the lady my father needed and convincing me my happiness lie in whatever was best for the family. My father could decide to allow me a few more weeks of childhood, but my mother had to make sure he got what he wanted when he wanted it. The whole thing sounded exhausting.

"You also have a lot of chores to get through," Gabriel reminded Embry.

"Does the month start now then?" Embry asked.

"A week is fine," Gabriel assured him.

"I guess I better leave..." Embry waited for Gabriel to tell him it was fine, that they would do double or nothing on the next bet.

"I'll see you tomorrow," I told him, as Gabriel was not letting him off.

"It might be afternoon. Late afternoon," he looked to Gabriel for pity.

"Godspeed," Gabriel told Embry, who sauntered off none too pleased.

"You're terrible," I said once we were alone.

"Are you forgetting when he had me muck out the stables for weeks?"

"I think the difference is that he beat you fair and square, whereas today..."

"You were the one who beat him," he finished for me. "But I bet on you, which is no different from..."

"From what?" I asked when he stopped himself.

"It's actually very different."

"From what?" I repeated.

"The time we bet on the rabbits."

"Oh, so I'm a rabbit?"

"Only in the sense that you are someone independent of us, that we bet on, even though neither of us could influence the outcome."

"He could have," I pointed out.

"Not against you," Gabriel smiled as we got to the bridge. My father paid his laborers extra to build it after I spent a summer crossing the divide by balancing on an overturned tree.

"Flattery gets you nowhere," I warned.

"Honestly, I would let him start any other day, but…"

"But what?" This time he didn't stop himself, he let the thought linger, as if I could guess what he meant to say.

"But I liked the idea of being able to walk the rest of the way home with you."

"Without him?" I asked.

"Without him," he agreed.

"I thought you had two best friends, Mr. Black."

"I do. But I have high hopes for one of them."

"What kind of hopes?" I asked. My heart was beating like it had at the top of the tree. My palms were sweaty, but I felt a shiver.

"Well, she's just a girl now, the kind with muddy boots, leaves in her hair and tears in her dresses--"

"Is something wrong with that?" I asked, ready to be offended if that was the case.

"Not a thing. I would have her stay that way forever."

"Just a girl?" For some reason, I didn't like that idea. I wanted all the liberties afforded to me as a girl, but when Gabriel smiled at me, I wanted to be one of those women in the beautiful dresses who go to a dance and fall in love.

"No, a beautiful lady who climbs trees and runs through puddles and laughs in a way that makes me feel like everything will always be okay, because nothing can be wrong when she smiles."

"She sounds nearly impossible to find," I could hear my heart pounding against my chest and had to remind myself to breathe.

"She would be. I can't imagine there's more than one of her in all of creation," he stopped on the edge of the forest that lines our property and turned to face me. "Luckily, I have found her, and she is standing right in front of me."

"She is," it came out as a cross between a question and a statement, as I got lost in his beautiful brown eyes. "I'm not..." I tried to come up with something clever.

"You're perfect," he said before leaning in so our lips were so close that I could nearly taste the strawberries we ate earlier. He wasn't coming any closer, so I bridged the distance. His lips met mine in a fabulous millisecond of magic.

CHAPTER 2

I had never been kissed like that before, so I had nothing to compare it to, but I was certain that no kiss could ever compare. Gabriel and Embry were both my best friends, but I had been in love with Gabriel for as long as I could remember.

"Annabelle!" my mother yelled from the front porch of our plantation house.

Technically, we were still hidden by the trees, but I nearly jumped out of my skin before stepping away so there were feet of distance between us.

"Don't worry, she can't see us," he assured me. He was smiling from ear to ear, like he just couldn't help it. "I've been wanting to do that forever," he admitted.

I swallowed hard before smiling back at him. "Me too," I agreed, but there was a sinking feeling in the pit of my stomach. Because he was my best friend, and that kiss was going to change things. For us, for Embry, for my parents...it changed everything.

"Come on," he put out his hand to bring me through the woods to the house, but I kept my hand to myself, shaking my head and motioning to where I knew my mother was standing, waiting for us. "Of course. Don't worry, I'll win her over," he winked before leading the way to the house. There was a bounce in his step that made my heart flutter.

"Good evening Mrs. Owens. How is the picnic coming along?" he asked once we got close. My mother was staring at us like she knew exactly what just happened. While I was a bunch of nerves, Gabriel attempted to normalize the situation.

"Will your father be at the picnic, Mr. Black?" my mother asked with the utmost politeness, though she held her head particularly high.

"He's been preparing for weeks," Gabriel assured her. "My mother's even made me a suit, in case there's dancing. It's very smart, quite like your husband's from last year's picnic," he was clearly trying to win her over, as he had promised, and I found it adorable. My mother, on the other hand, was not so impressed.

"You should be heading home," she told him, making it a point to look out at the setting sun. "It's getting late."

"Of course. Have a lovely evening, Mrs. Owens," he bowed to her before turning to me. "I'll see you tomorrow?" he asked with a smile.

"I'll see you tomorrow," I couldn't help but return his smile. I could feel how red and flushed my face was.

"Go wash up, Annabelle," my mother told me when I got to our porch. I looked back to Gabriel, who turned as he was walking to give me one last smile.

"Of course, mama," I gave her a kiss on the cheek before going inside and trying to remove any evidence of climbing the tree and splashing adventures in the creek.

CHAPTER 3

My father's partner and his wife, whom I called Uncle Robert and Aunt Elena, were invited to dine with us, so most of the dinner conversation revolved around them and their business ventures, leaving me to sit in my own world, trying to think straight while I could still feel the imprint of Gabriel's lips on mine.

I thought I was doing a wonderful job of participating just enough in the conversation that no one would get suspicious, but Aunt Elena found me in my room once the adults went to the sitting room for a night cap.

"Is everything okay?" she asked, gently knocking on my door, not waiting for my response before letting herself in. She and Uncle Robert had three boys who were all grown up, so she had always treated me a bit like the daughter she never had. I'm fairly certain it bothered my mother, who got jealous whenever Aunt Elena did something motherly towards me, but I didn't mind.

"Of course," I gave her what I hoped was a convincing smile, but she sort of squinted at me before coming to sit beside me on the bed.

"Anything on your mind?" she pressed.

"The picnic is coming up. And the summer's almost over."

They were trivial events. We were literally talking about the weather, but she nodded in understanding.

"Is this about climbing trees, or the boys you do it with?" My shocked expression made her laugh. "You shouldn't go so high if you don't want to be seen," she reproached.

"I had to," I said with utter conviction.

"Because..." It wasn't that she didn't believe me, but she could tell it was more arbitrary than a gun to my head that forced me to do it.

"Embry thought I couldn't do it," I admitted, aware that wasn't a good enough reason to defy my parents.

"What about Gabriel?" she asked.

"What about him?"

"Did he think you could do it?"

My feelings were either written on my face or she could read minds, something I had often suspected of her.

"He did, but I had to prove it to Embry, and to myself."

"You needed to defend your own honor," she said simply.

She didn't say anything else, but she sighed and looked over to me, waiting with a small, compassionate smile.

"He kissed me," I admitted, feeling the flush in my cheeks and the smile that I couldn't stop.

"Gabriel," she said like there was no other option.

"How do you know?"

"Your face lights up when you talk about him. If Embry kissed you, there would be less smiling and more dread."

"Embry is my best friend," I argued.

"Oh, he's wonderful. But I'm sure even he knows you're in love with Gabriel, and to do anything like that would mean destroying his two most important friendships."

"You're saying everyone knows?" I asked.

"Everyone who pays attention," she agreed.

"My mother?" I asked.

"What's wrong?" she asked instead of answering.

I sighed before coming clean. "When he kissed me, it was like...fireworks," I smiled, bringing my fingers to my lips and remembering it.

"The best ones are," she agreed.

"But then I realized that it changes everything," I continued, her smile not helping. "We can't stay best friends who occasionally kiss. And as soon as we tell Embry, things will be weird..."

"And more importantly..." she pressed when I didn't.

"My mother doesn't approve. At all. My father hasn't said anything, but I doubt he feels differently," I admitted.

"What do you want in all of this?" she asked me.

"Gabriel," I said simply. "But I also want things to stay the same. To climb trees and run around with both him and Embry, until I'm older and we get married and live happily ever after," I added, not expecting it when she laughed at me. "It isn't funny."

"No, but it is familiar," she assured me.

"What did you do?" I asked.

"I waited for him to grow up," she shrugged.

"I don't think it's his age she has a problem with," I argued.

"No, I think it's a boy being interested in her little girl."

"Growing up won't change that. I hope," I added the last part worriedly, but even the thought of Gabriel not being there for me seemed ridiculous. He'd been there the first day I set foot on American soil and hadn't left my side since. No matter what I was going through, or what happened in the world around us, he always felt like home. A strong, stable, solid presence that made me feel safe, yet also gave me butterflies. I brought my hand to the scar on my right palm, remembering the day I got it, trying to impress him in my father's study. Gabriel bandaged it and kissed my broken skin, setting my world on fire. But that was Gabriel. Taking care of me and knowing exactly what to do. I remember thinking I would take another wound if it gave me another kiss.

"I don't think so either," Aunt Elena smiled. "But right now Gabriel is a boy your mother knows as the reason you come home with tousled hair, torn stockings and muddy boots."

"It's not his fault. Or Embry's. I know she wants me to be prim and proper, but she has no idea what it is like at the top of the trees, or how good it feels to splash around in the creek on a hot summer day."

"I didn't know your mother at your age, but I daresay she knows exactly what being young, innocent and carefree feels like," Aunt Elena said, her eyes drifting off as if she was remembering when she was a little girl.

"So once I stop acting like a child, you think she'll approve of Gabriel?" I asked hopefully.

"Once you start acting like the lady she wants you to be, and he becomes the man who deserves you, I'm sure she'll approve."

"She might be more interested in a man who can tame me."

I got her to laugh, but this time it was on purpose. "Give him a chance. I've seen him in town. He's been following Dr. Smith around since he cured Patrick, and I believe he has big dreams. Let them come true," she suggested. I shuddered at the memory of the time we thought Gabriel's little brother was going to die. Gabriel had been reading up and asking questions about everything related to medicine ever since.

"There you are, Annabelle. Stop bothering Mrs. Archer.

Your father would love for you to sing for us," my mother barged in and expertly disguised her shock at finding Aunt Elena and I sharing secrets in my bedroom.

"Of course, mama," I went over and kissed her on the cheek before going downstairs.

CHAPTER 4

Once Aunt Elena and Uncle Robert went home, I found myself lingering outside my father's study, pacing back and forth in the hallway. I knew Aunt Elena was right, that the best thing I could do was nothing. Gabriel knew how my mother was, so he would have to understand that we had to stay friends for now, until I could convince my parents he was my perfect match. But at the same time, I didn't want to wait. I loved him, and I didn't care who knew it.

"Annabelle," my father called, just as I brought my fist up to knock on his door.

"Yes, papa?" I asked, trying to steady my heart and slow my breathing. My nerves were making me look guilty, although I knew I hadn't done anything wrong.

"Were you in the hallway?" he asked, crinkling his eyebrows at me.

"I was coming to say goodnight," I lied. He seemed nervous, which couldn't be good.

"I was talking to your mother," he began, coming around to sit at the edge of his desk.

"About the picnic?" I asked hopefully when he stopped

there, but he took off his glasses and pinched the bridge of his nose.

"I know we agreed you could spend one last summer doing things that could be considered inappropriate for a daughter of mine..."

"Until classes start again," I agreed.

"Of course," he smiled, but there was something dismissive about it. I knew a lot of my classmates weren't returning in the fall, as they were going to work or get married instead, but I had hoped I wouldn't be one of them. "But your mother and I were talking, and the picnic is a big event that launches the social season, and..."

"And it's my last summer picnic." I knew where he was going, but it was taking him forever, and I hoped he might lose his resolve.

"You'll have so many summer picnics, my darling." He put his hand out, so I gave him mine, and he pulled me into him. "We had a beautiful dress made for you, and I think it would be nice if I could present you to society without grass stains on your skirts and mud on your cheek."

"I can be careful," I offered. "It's really just races, and..." even as I said the words, I knew it was useless. Reluctant or not, his decision was made.

"You're too old to be running around and gallivanting with those boys, my love."

"Is this about dresses or Embry and Gabriel?" I asked, careful not to show any emotion as I said their names.

"It's about both, as it's about neither. They all represent your childhood, but it's time to grow up, Annabelle. You're not a child anymore."

"Are you saying I can't be friends with them anymore?" I asked, my heart almost stopping in my chest.

"Of course not. You'll see them in town and you can be friendly, but it's not normal for a lady to spend all of her time with boys." For the first time this conversation, he looked at me with certainty. His answer was final.

"Yes, father," I said blankly. "Goodnight." I tried to hold my emotions in until I could get to my room and be alone.

"Goodnight, Annabelle," he dismissed me.

I WENT to bed and stared at the ceiling, thinking how much things could change in a matter of hours, or in an instant. That afternoon I was enjoying one of my last carefree days of summer. Then Gabriel kissed me and it took me out of my comfort zone, into a world of scary possibilities. Now I was alone, my carefree days over, and things would never be the same again. I was dreading the dress I would have to wear and the conversations I would have to fake, but more than anything, I was dreading what this meant for me and Gabriel. Not only was a relationship completely out of the question now, I wasn't even sure we could be friends.

CHAPTER 5

"Miss Owens," Gabriel walked over and did a fancy bow when he ran into Eugenia and I at the picnic. I'd heard my mother telling him I couldn't go out and play with him anymore when he came to the house, but I hadn't seen him since he'd kissed me. My breath caught in my chest at the sight of him in his new suit, but I tried my best not to show it.

"Mr. Black," I overexaggerated my curtsey.

"Miss Monroe," he acknowledged my companion before turning back to me. "I trust you're enjoying the festivities?"

"You'll have to congratulate your brother for me, on his excellent marksmanship," I said, as Patrick had claimed the first-place ribbon. Normally, I would have competed with the boys, never coming close to winning, but still having a wonderful time. My parents were right though; I would have been the oldest girl there by far if I had participated.

"We're all very proud of him," he assured me. I could already feel everything shifting. He was looking at me the way he always had, but his words were guarded, analyzing the optics before saying or doing anything.

"Congratulations to you as well," Eugenia chimed in. "Fastest man in Boston."

"The last sober man at the picnic," he was always modest, implying it had less to do with skill, and everything to do with drinking habits.

"Aren't you ladies a lovely sight for sore eyes," Embry arrived, draping an arm around Gabriel's shoulder.

"Oh, Embry, what have you done to your hair?" I asked. There was a gold ribbon tied in it, as well as what looked like twigs and dead leaves.

"A gentleman doesn't kiss and tell," he smiled to me.

The four of us stood there awkwardly for a moment. Eugenia was trying to weigh her chances with both of my best friends, while I was struggling to resist rushing into their arms. With Gabriel officially apprenticing for Dr. Smith now, Embry working with his brother, and my father's thinly-veiled warning... I doubted I would have another chance to.

"We were on our way home, if the two of you wouldn't mind accompanying us," Eugenia broke the silence.

"It would be our pleasure," Embry assured her, breaking the ice as he fell in line between us, leaving Gabriel the spot on my right.

"Why are you leaving so early?" he asked me while Eugenia talked to Embry about his sister, Maria, who was teaching her how to play the viola, without much success.

"There isn't so much to see when you're not allowed to do any of it," I explained. "Why did you leave?"

"Perhaps I was waiting for you?"

I could feel my cheeks blushing. "That would be quite inappropriate, Mr. Black," I warned.

"In that case we'll say I had business to get to," he said, his brown eyes studying my face like he was trying to see the truth behind my polite exterior. With those eyes, I believed he could.

CHAPTER 6

The next time I saw Gabriel outside of church was a few months later, as I was getting ready for yet another social engagement, where my mother would introduce me to all of the eligible bachelors, and I would do my best to be equally polite and annoying, so none of them would want to stick around. I was walking down the stairs so my mother could help me with the final touches, but instead I found Gabriel in the foyer.

"You look...breathtaking." he said, making me blush more than I already was. My dress was deep green, like a luscious forest. He was in awe, nearly speechless, but his eyes were full of yearning and remorse.

"Are you coming to the dance?" My heart beat faster and my stomach was in knots.

"No, I came to see your father. Purely business," he gave me a smile, that told me it was anything but. His eyes had a sadness to them.

"Purely?" I tried to get his eyes to smile along.

"Perhaps I hoped I would be lucky enough to see you before you left."

"And this doesn't change your mind?" I asked, twirling for him. The words had my usual confidence, but inside I was nothing but nerves. Around Gabriel, of all people. It made no sense, but every time he came close, I was overrun by a mix of emotions that, while confusing, I did not want to stop.

"About attending?" His eyes never left me, going back and forth between my dress and my eyes, both making me blush.

"I am certain you were invited," I agreed.

"I really must speak with your father," he argued. I was so fixated on my own nerves that I hadn't noticed his.

"Is everything okay?" I asked.

"Of course, Bells. Just some boring forms to sign."

"He's in the study. Bookkeeping, I believe, so your forms will fit right in."

"Thank you." There was nothing silly about his bow today, but his eyes did linger on me, taking one last look at my dress before he went down the hallway.

"WHO WAS THAT?" my mother asked, bringing me the pearl earrings she wanted me to wear.

"Gabriel Black," I said like I couldn't care less. "These are beautiful." The earrings were simple, but I had never seen such big, white pearls before.

"They were my mother's. I never felt comfortable wearing them here, but you look like a princess," she told me proudly.

"The dress is lovely," I was grateful. Tonight was a big event, and I knew how much effort she put into it for me.

"No, you're lovely, and the dress is lucky to be on you," she gave me a smile before adjusting my hair.

"Thank you, mama," I told her.

"One day you'll have a daughter of your own and you'll understand," she told me.

"We should get going," I went over to grab my coat. I was

truly grateful, and did feel like a princess tonight. It wasn't that getting married and having children scared me. I had long ago resigned myself to being the lady and wife I knew I had to become, but I did not want to meet him tonight, which I knew was her dream.

"I'll go get your father," she smiled at me before she went, but it didn't reach her eyes. Our relationship had been strained for years, and I had always been a daddy's girl, but I still remembered when her arms around me were the only thing that made me feel safe. Which was why her polite smile to cover her hurt broke my heart.

"WE CAN DROP you off on the way," my mother was offering when she returned with my father and Gabriel at her heels.

"Oh, that won't be necessary. I can walk," Gabriel assured her.

"You're not attending?" my father asked, surprised.

"It's not really my—"

"He can't go wearing—"

My mother and Gabriel both tried to dissuade him, but my father's mind was immovable once he made it up. "Nonsense, you can wear my jacket. If you're looking to establish yourself, you need more than excellent grades, Gabriel. You need to know people, and tonight will be full of people.

"The very best people," I added with a smile I wouldn't have been able to stop, even if I had tried.

"That's the spirit," my father put his hand on my shoulder before Gabriel followed him to get a jacket, leaving me alone with my mother.

"I thought Gabriel was a laborer," she interrupted the silence.

"He's apprenticing with Dr. Smith so he can some day take over and treat people."

"That doctor is a godsend," she said. I could almost see the wheels spinning in her brain.

"I heard Gabriel is a fast learner who has proven to be incredibly helpful." I spent a lot of my time casually bringing up all of Gabriel's achievements in an attempt to get a reaction from her. She tended to focus on any bad rumors about him and Embry, completely ignoring anything that painted them in a decent light.

"Winter months are when help will be needed. It's not even November yet and the cold is already moving in," she looked out the window as if she could see it happening.

CHAPTER 7

My father and Gabriel talked business on the ride, then left to make introductions once we arrived. I let my mother fix my hair one last time before going over to Eugenia and Maria, who were patiently waiting to be introduced to society.

"I was hoping he would be here," Eugenia said excitedly, looking over my shoulder as I sat down beside her.

"Who?" I asked, turning to where she was looking. "Gabriel?"

"Gabriel Black makes me weak in the knees. I nearly trip over my own feet every time he's near me."

"I had no idea," I said, looking around at the other girls my age. Some of them had grown up with us, while others I had never seen before, but they all noticed him. Most looked at him like he was a delicious piece of cake they wanted very badly, but couldn't have, while the new faces were intrigued, whispering amongst themselves about who he might be.

"Embry is adorable as well, but there's something about tall, dark and handsome that I can't resist," Eugenia defended herself.

He is irresistible, I thought to myself. But I always hoped the other girls wouldn't notice.

EUGENIA WAS the first of us onto the dance floor, with Mr. Roosevelt, one of the rich merchants from the city. He'd just bought the property across the grounds from ours and, while he was at least a decade older than us, he had a kind smile and bright green eyes that gave him a youthful air. I also knew, from occasionally wandering where I shouldn't, that he was an absolute gentleman when he found women on their own in the middle of a forest.

"I'm starving to death," I confided in Maria. I usually ate before coming, but Gabriel had shown up and distracted me. I could practically feel my stomach digesting itself.

"Surely you won't die?" she asked with concern.

"Of course not. I just mean that I'm hungry," I assured her. She had a tendency to take me literally, which I assumed came from her having to translate everything into Italian in her mind. Embry had moved here when he was a little boy, but his older siblings had joined after my family was already settled.

"I'm certain I saw a table with some –"

"That's quite alright, Maria, I'll eat when I get home." I knew that no matter what was on that table, my mother would not approve of me eating it here, in front of everyone.

She looked at me with confusion before Eugenia returned to us from the dance floor.

"Escorted home by Embry Dante and asked to dance by Mr. Roosevelt, what is your secret?" Maria asked her.

"He reminds me of my brother," Eugenia did a face that implied she had no interest in the wealthy Mr. Roosevelt, before her eyes found Gabriel across the dance floor. He was still talking with my father and a group of men whose daughters were on the dance floor.

"Miss Owens," a voice I didn't recognize said from behind us, summoning me away from Gabriel. "My name is Bartholomew Mayweather. I was hoping I could have this dance," he asked, extending his hand to help me to my feet.

I looked over to Gabriel, who was busy talking to Uncle Robert, then to my mother, whose smile urged me to accept him.

"It would be my pleasure," I nodded.

He moved gracefully and followed the music perfectly, but he didn't talk. Nor was he very forthcoming when I asked him questions, getting nothing more than he was new to Boston and renting a small cottage while his estate was being built.

"Are you with any family?" I asked. He didn't look much older than me, so I doubted he moved to town on his own.

"My parents. We came tonight for my sister." He nodded over to a timid girl of maybe thirteen, who tried, unsuccessfully, to hide her red hair with a dark brown bonnet.

"And what is it you do?" I asked him.

"We own ships."

"Sounds interesting. What kinds of ships?" I tried my best to be polite and interested, but he made it incredibly difficult.

"We lease them."

"To pirates?" I teased, hoping to get a smile. He had a foot and a half on me and was staunchly looking ahead. He was either bored or distracted.

"Pirates are not a laughing matter," he warned. "And they would never pay for a ship. By their very definition, they take them."

"Of course. I'm sorry, I don't know much about ships and was—"

"No one would expect you to," he assured me in what felt like a very condescending manner, before he put his concentration back on the dance.

I WAS INCREDIBLY grateful when the music finally ended, so I could bow out of that encounter. I was heading back to Eugenia, to warn her to stay clear of Mr. Mayweather, when Gabriel was suddenly in front of me, smiling.

"I see you've managed to escape my father's companions," I returned his smile while doing a slight curtsey.

"Just in time, by the looks of it," he nodded off to my previous dance partner, who was now talking to Maria. "May I have the honor of escorting you to the dance floor?" he asked of me.

"I assure you, the honor is mine, Dr. Black."

"Let's not get ahead of ourselves," he warned, trying to disguise his smile. "Your father has been most helpful."

"He loves helping people," I assured him. "Plus, it's good for him if years from now, he's in the good graces of the town's very prominent doctor."

"He knows he would never have to worry about that."

"He can be cutthroat in business when he has to be."

"He's still your father," he argued. "No matter how he treated me, he would always receive the utmost of my capabilities, because of what it would do to you to lose him."

"Well, you've certainly garnered an audience," I changed the subject, focusing on the people around the room rather than on his words.

"Where?" he looked around like he didn't even see them.

"You must have noticed. Every girl in here is looking at you like you're—"

"I'm too busy looking at you," he cut me off.

"You were busy putting yourself in the good graces of every member of high society my father could spot."

"I don't know if it will be enough, but it certainly won't hurt," he agreed, sounding surprised. As was I.

"What were the forms for?"

"Are we really going to talk about your father's business?" He twirled me around the floor with a skill I did not expect him to have. My heart was beating a mile a minute, and this wasn't helping.

"What else did you want to talk about?" I was nervous, which I attributed to the inner battle I was going through, of wanting more than anything for him to kiss me, while also knowing that I would die if he did it here, in front of everyone, including my parents.

"All of the eligible bachelors vying for your affections this evening, how beautiful you look in this dress, how easily one could get lost in your eyes…"

"Normal, everyday conversations," I summed it up.

"Always," he agreed with his smile, the one that feels like home and melted all my nerves away.

"You have no competition here," I assured him of all the eligible bachelors. "Mr. Mayweather is a bore who believes I am too simple to comprehend too many words."

"I'm sure one of them will be charming and respectful and check all the boxes your mother has for you." The words weren't meant to be comforting. He knew it was only a matter of time before my parents found me someone worthy of carrying on my father's legacy.

"Even then," I locked eyes with his, seeing mostly sadness reflected in them.

"Bells…" He kept an appropriate distance from me, but just the heat of his palm on mine sent shivers down my spine.

"You're going to be a doctor, Gabriel. No one could say you aren't worthy."

"Your mother still sees me as the boy you snuck out in the middle of the night to chase fireflies with."

"Are you turning me down or warning me not to get my hopes up?" I asked.

"What are you proposing?" He grinned, but there was a sadness behind it.

"To wait. As long as I make myself undesirable enough, you'll go to medical school and become a doctor, at which point my parents would be crazy to do anything other than welcome you into the family with open arms."

"See, right there, that's a terrible plan."

"Why?"

"How in the world could you ever make yourself undesirable?" he asked before the music ended, and my father summoned him once more, either for further introductions, or because of the way he was looking at me.

"I'M sorry about all those things I said earlier," Eugenia said once I followed her to the gardens for some air.

"What did you say?" I asked, wondering if she had complained to Maria about me when I wasn't paying attention.

"About Gabriel."

"I don't remember you saying anything rude about him," I argued. Everything she said just told me that he could have his pick of women if he didn't still have his eye on me.

"Nothing rude, but I didn't realize the two of you were—"

"We're not," I stopped her before she could go any further, but she just looked at me with the compassion Aunt Elena usually gave me.

"I saw the way you danced together."

"We're old friends," I argued.

"Take this from someone who has spent the entire evening watching him; he has not taken his eyes off you. Whether he was talking with old men or fending off flirtatious smiles, his eyes always found you."

"I hadn't noticed."

"He mostly waited until you were no longer staring at him," she gave me a smile.

"I'm sorry," I apologized to her.

"Don't be silly, Annabelle, he's my tall, dark and handsome, but he's your soulmate," she said with certainty.

"Embry is incredible," I offered with a smile.

"You're not the first to say it," she assured me.

"Really?" I asked.

"He has quite the following." She raised her eyebrow suggestively and I couldn't help but giggle. "But I think I'll give Mr. Roosevelt a chance.

"I didn't think you liked him."

"Not when I thought I had a chance with Gabriel, but he's...he's kind," she decided, and I knew exactly what she meant.

"You have my full support if he's what you want, but you deserve someone who isn't just kind to you. You deserve someone who sets your heart on fire. Or at the very least, makes you smile," I told her.

"So do you," she replied, looking over to where Gabriel was talking to my Aunt Elena. "You should go to him," she told me as Mr. Roosevelt approached us.

I WAS MAKING my way to Gabriel, but was surprised to see my father in the courtyard with who I believed to be Bartholomew's father. I had no idea that they knew each other.

"When you asked me here, I thought you had a business proposal," my father did not sound impressed.

"Not in the strictest sense of the word, but I do have a proposition," he paused to gauge my father's interest, but I could picture my father's stony business face, which usually revealed nothing.

I don't know why I didn't walk over and let them know I was there, but I hid behind a rose bush and eavesdropped instead.

"I wanted to ask you for Annabelle's hand in marriage. For my son," he said as simply as if he were purchasing a loaf of bread. I was shocked, having assumed Bartholomew found me as boring as I found him.

"You want him to marry my daughter?" my father sounded confused. "Have they even met?"

"Yes, they danced earlier, and I spoke with your wife. I am told she is an accomplished singer who speaks multiple languages."

"My daughter or my wife?" my father made a joke, giving himself the chance to process the question. Mr. Mayweather's expression remained unchanged.

"We have a very lucrative shipping business and though he will be required to travel back to England on occasion, this will be his home base. Your daughter is beautiful and pleasant to talk to, and he would like to marry her."

"While I am flattered by the interest," my father paused, in complete control of the conversation. "I'm afraid there have been many libations this evening, and you'll have to wait for an answer in the morning."

"Of course, Mr. Owens, take your time." Mr. Mayweather's words did not match his tone. "Bartholomew will be in your neighborhood tomorrow afternoon, if that's suitable?"

"That should be fine," my father was non-committal, but it was clearly the end of the conversation.

I hurried back to the garden just in time to watch Mr. Mayweather return to the music inside, followed a few minutes later by my father.

"THERE YOU ARE," Gabriel found me still leaning against a tree, with my hand pressed to my heart. "I grew worried when Eugenia returned and you were—"

I silenced him by wrapping my arms around his waist and holding him close, something I hadn't done so openly in years.

"What's wrong? Did someone hurt you?" he asked.

Everything I needed to know about him I could hear in those words; his concern and love for me, what he would do to anyone who dared hurt me, and the promise that I would always be safe with him.

"It's nothing. I just needed a moment." I stepped back from him and tried to smile like everything was okay, but this changed everything. We couldn't just wait for Gabriel to become a physician so he could be an acceptable prospect for my parents. I had to do something now.

"Are you sure?" he asked me, knowing I was lying, but giving me the benefit of the doubt.

"It will be," I assured him with a more convincing smile this time. "You're working with Dr. Smith this week?"

"As soon as I'm done at the factory," he agreed.

"What time do you usually finish at?"

"Eight or nine, it depends how many patients he has to see. Though he always takes Wednesdays off," he volunteered.

"Can you meet me on Baker street as soon as you're done work on Wednesday?"

"Should I ask what this is all about?"

"Will it change your answer?" I turned it on him.

"I will see you on Wednesday," he shook his head like he found me impossible.

I tried to tease him back, even sticking out my tongue when no one was looking, but it felt like my heart was being compressed by a ton of rocks, and the whole structure was about to crumble on me.

"Everything will be okay," he assured me, reaching for my hand and giving it a squeeze.

"Of course it will."

He knew I wasn't convinced, just like I knew he had no way of knowing anything would be okay, but when he held my hand, I felt like it would be.

CHAPTER 8

The following morning, I got up early and made myself a tea, then waited at the kitchen table until I heard my father's footsteps on the stairs.

"Would you like some tea?" I called up to him.

"You're up early?" he said, coming into the kitchen.

"I couldn't sleep," I chose honesty, but didn't tell him why.

"I would love some," he decided.

"Shall I bring it to your office?"

"I think I have time to enjoy breakfast with my daughter," he assured me, taking a seat at the table.

I poured him a cup of tea, then made a plate of scones and biscuits, with some homemade jam.

"You spoil me," he said when I put it down in front of him.

"It might be a bribe," I admitted, taking a seat.

"You know I can't say no to you, sweets or not."

I waited until he put half the scone in his mouth before saying, "I heard you and Mr. Mayweather last night."

"Perhaps *I* should have made *you* breakfast," he gave me a sad smile.

"You're going to say yes?" I asked, not expecting how heartbroken it made me feel that he cared so little about my happiness.

"Ultimately the decision would be yours," he told me. "I spoke with your mother and we were going to give him our blessing, but I would never force you to accept a proposal you didn't want to."

I believed him. He would never force me to say yes. But I was raised better than to go against him, so as soon as he gave his blessing, my fate would be sealed.

"Could you ask for more time?"

"Time for what?"

"As soon as he asks me, with your blessing, I would say yes." He gave me the courtesy of not pretending it wasn't true. "I'm not asking you to say no, papa, I understand that he's wealthy and powerful and I'm sure mama could tell me all about him," I smiled so it didn't seem like I was blaming her for organizing this. "But I don't know him. I barely spent five minutes with him last night, and I would love it if you could ask for more time to make your decision, so that I can get to know him," I rambled and lost the rehearsed speech I'd been reciting in my head all morning.

"How much time?"

"A couple of months?" I asked. It wasn't nearly enough time for what I had planned, but it was more than he would be willing to give me.

"I'm sure a month would be sufficient to know his character," he countered.

"A month then," I agreed.

"And when this month is over, you'll say yes and be happy with him?" he verified.

I didn't want to lie to him, so I chose my words carefully, "If, at the end of the month, you give him your blessing, then

I will say yes to Bartholomew's proposal and try my best to be happy."

"Then I'll see what I can do," he assured me.

"Thank you, papa." I gave him a kiss on the cheek.

"Can we still have breakfast, or was it really just a bribe?"

"I would love some breakfast." I smiled at him before grabbing a scone and smothering it with jam.

"WHAT'S HAPPENING HERE?" my mother asked when she walked in and found us giggling.

"Nothing, my dear. Just telling Annabelle that Bartholomew will be coming over this afternoon. It should be an excellent opportunity for her to get to know him," he winked at me.

"He's a wonderful young man," she sat beside me at the table and took my hands in hers. "I met him on the way home from picking up your dress last week. He was heading into town and found me right after we got stuck in a mudslide. He asked if he could help and I told him yes, once you get to town, please tell my husband to send someone for me—"

"I heard nothing of this," my father cut in.

"Yes, I told you last night."

"You told me you met him, but I did not hear about a mudslide."

"I didn't need to tell you, because Bartholomew took care of it. He got out of his carriage and used his own hands to push us out."

"As opposed to someone else's hands?" I asked.

"What?" she was confused until my father laughed, and she understood what I had said. "Oh, you laugh, but he saved me from spending hours waiting for someone else to come by. Most men in his position would have just gone to your father, or sent someone else to take care of it."

"You're right. That was very nice of him," I said apologetically. "I'll be sure to thank him for it this afternoon."

"Give him a chance," she urged me.

"I will," I promised.

BARTHOLOMEW WAS BROUGHT straight to my father's study when he arrived. It took all of my self-restraint not to wait outside the door and eavesdrop as I had last night, but I trusted my father, and my mother was already suspicious enough.

"Miss Owens," Bartholomew said when he came out what felt like an eternity later.

"Mr. Mayweather," I greeted him.

"I have heard that your father's gardens are like a work of art. Would you care to show them to me?"

"It would be my pleasure," I assured him, but my mother was the only one whose smile was genuine.

CHAPTER 9

On Wednesday I waited for Gabriel outside of Mr. Cole's shop. They were closing soon, but he agreed to stay a bit late to take some measures for me, although I'm not sure how much longer he was going to wait. My mother certainly kept him occupied, but he was the best tailor in Boston.

"Is this an adventure or a conversation?" Gabriel asked from behind me. Even before he spoke, there was an electricity in the air that gave me shivers.

"Both," I said, turning around to face him. "You're late."

"One of the guys in the shipping yard cut himself, so his buddy thought he would be funny and brought him to me instead of the foreman," he gave his excuse.

"How did you do?" I asked. As far as excuses went, his was pretty valid.

"I don't think he'll lose the finger, and the foreman said I had a physician-like precision."

"Makes sense, as you're a future physician," I smiled at the exhilaration on his face, from the adrenaline that hadn't quite died down yet.

"Hopefully," he agreed. "What are we doing this evening?"

"Our first stop is Mr. Cole," I explained, letting him inside the shop.

"This is your friend?" Mr. Cole asked me, eying him up and down.

"Yes, this is Gabriel Black," I introduced him.

"I know the Blacks," he assured me. "Is this for any particular occasion?"

"Just something he can wear day to day while assisting Dr. Smith. Perhaps something that could be used for important house calls as well as dinner parties."

"What are you talking about?" Gabriel asked me.

"I have the latest fashions from Paris," Mr. Cole tried to entice me.

"Leave those for my father. We're looking for something more traditional here. Elderly people with weak hearts, you see," I turned him down.

"Of course, Miss Owens. I'll be right back." He ran off to a back room.

Gabriel's eyes were still on me, waiting for an explanation.

"This is the adventure part."

"I can see that. What I don't see is how I am going to pay for a new wardrobe on a laborer's salary while also saving for medical school and—"

"It's my treat," I said, even though he was looking at me like his next words would be about his plans to marry me and provide me with the life I deserved.

"I can't accept that," he argued.

"Of course you can," I assured him.

"I never realized it bothered you," he was offended.

"It doesn't," I said, bridging the distance so I could put my hand on his arm. "At the ball, someone asked my father for my hand in marriage."

"Congratulations," the hurt in his eyes destroyed me, while the rest of his face tried to look happy for me.

"I convinced my father to give me a month. I said it was so I could get to know my suitor, but…"

"But what, Annabelle?" he was so close, and his eyes were locked on mine.

"When you kissed me in the woods…" I said, very aware of my voice shaking.

"Before your parents decided we were no longer allowed to 'run around' with you outside of school," he let me know he hadn't forgotten.

"I told you to do it again someday."

"That wasn't some veiled way of turning me down without crushing my feelings?"

"No, it was me trying to find a way to save you from my parents without losing you."

"You'll never lose me, Annabelle. No matter who you marry or where you go, you will always have me."

"I know," I brought my hand to his cheek and gave a weak smile. "But I don't just want you as my best friend. I don't want to dance with you on the side while my husband talks to his friends, or spend the rest of my life wishing I was with you. Because I do. I want to be with you," I told him.

"But I have to look the part?" he focused on our adventure rather than my words.

"I thought that as soon as you became a doctor, they would have no choice but to welcome you like the son they always wanted."

"It doesn't work like that," he argued.

"No, it doesn't, because my father is only giving me a month, and that is not enough time."

"So you're going to turn me into what they want for you, in the hopes that they'll finally accept me?" he asked.

"The last thing I want to do is change you, Gabriel. As far

as I'm concerned, you're perfect. You have the biggest heart, you're hardworking and smart and my heart beats faster at the thought of you…but I need you to look like them, so they can see it."

"Bells…" he still wasn't convinced.

"Do you love me?" I asked, suddenly nervous.

"With all my heart," he said without hesitation.

"This is my own money that I have saved, and I want to spend it on you, because I will never forgive myself if I didn't do everything in my power to make sure I got the happily ever after I have always wanted."

"With me?" he verified.

"There has never been anyone else, Gabriel. There never will be." I assured him.

"Then I will do whatever you need me to," he promised.

Mr. Cole came back with a large package and the measuring tape around his neck. After confirming a few sizes, he opened the package to reveal three gorgeous suits.

"They were ordered months ago for Mr. Lemming, but they won't be fitting him any time soon," Mr. Cole delicately. Mrs. Lemming passed away over the winter and Mr. Lemming was not taking it very well at all. He was hardly seen outside of the house they once shared, and every time he was spotted, he was substantially larger than the time before. It was like he spent his days eating to try and fill the void his wife's death left him with.

"They're beautiful," I told Mr. Cole.

"You're a bit shorter than he was, so I'll have to hem the pant a bit, but if you don't mind that they weren't custom made for you, I can sell you the lot of them for a shilling," he offered.

"That would be incredibly kind, and I would be grateful," Gabriel told him.

"I should have them ready by Friday," Mr. Cole assured us.

"I'll bring the money with me," Gabriel promised.

"You can't afford those," I reproached once we were outside.

"I can pick up some extra shifts," he said like it wasn't a big deal, but I knew that it was. "If I want to prove to your father that I deserve you, I can't let you buy me suits to impress him. I don't want to trick him, I want him to see that I am the man for you. That I will love you every single day for the rest of my life, and I will provide for you, so you can live the life you deserve."

"All I want is you," I argued.

"But you deserve the world." He brought my hand to his lips and kissed it, causing a shock right through to my heart.

CHAPTER 10

My father's influence helped, and people started requesting Gabriel for house calls when Dr. Smith was unavailable. Sometimes even instead of him. He was maintaining his hours at the factory, but also accompanying Dr. Smith more and more. He was meeting influential people and showing them his competence, which had me overly confident with my plan, especially now that I knew for sure that Gabriel was on board with it.

Bartholomew, on the other hand, seemed to have taken my father's request for time to heart. He showed up every three days, just before lunch, so I could get to know him better. A combination of his boring personality and his displeasure with the wait resulted in the most dreadful meals in his company. If this continued any longer, I wouldn't be surprised if he turned even my mother against him as well.

I was prepared for another meal in silence, followed by an afternoon of boredom, when Bartholomew walked in with his parents and younger sister.

"You brought your family." I made an effort to smile.

"Yes, your mother recommended it. Although I dare say my mother has been just as eager to get to know my fiancée."

I tried to argue and remind him that there had been no proposal, no blessings given, and I would hopefully never be his fiancée, but my mother came and wrapped her arm around me, ushering us toward the backyard.

"I'm sure Annabelle would love to show your parents our gardens," she volunteered me.

"Oh, that would be lovely," his sister said excitedly.

"I've heard the gardens are a sight to behold," his mother said, louder than necessary, probably in the hopes of summoning my father from his office. He'd been cooped up in there all morning, upset about some accounts. He was being incredibly secretive around my mother and I, who both couldn't care less about his business.

"Why doesn't Annabelle give you a quick tour while I make sure lunch is ready?"

"I doubt a quick tour would be satisfying. I would much rather sit down and catch up so we may enjoy the extent of it after lunch," Mrs. Mayweather argued.

"Of course," my mother nodded to her before going to check on lunch, while I brought everyone into the sitting room. Mr. Mayweather immediately took to examining all of the paintings on the wall, while Mrs. Mayweather observed me like a farmer observed an animal at auction; a little crazy was okay, as long as I had wide enough hips to birth children, and the manners to hide it from strangers.

I sought refuge in his sister, Edith, who was enthralled by our harpsichord.

"Do you play?" she asked me.

"I sing mostly," I said, sitting beside her.

"Mother never lets me sing. Barry loves the viola, so she let me try it once, but she thinks I have no rhythm."

"Maybe you just have your own," I suggested.

"Isn't that the same thing?"

"No. Some things are beautiful, even if the world doesn't agree on it. My father finds me stuffy and out of tune whenever I play sheet music, but some days I'll just play around and do my own thing and he says it sounds beautiful."

"And you believe him?" she asked, looking over to her own father.

"I do," I smiled at her. "He rarely tells me in the moment. Usually it's at the next party, when he'll ask me to play that piece I was rehearsing the other day, and I have nothing to offer."

"Can you play all of these?" she asked, flipping the pages of sheet music, quickly tucking a loose strand of red hair back into her bonnet.

"I've learnt them all, but there are only a very few I can play well."

"Is this you?" she said, making me turn to see a full-page rendition of my face.

"It is," I agreed, hoping my emotions wouldn't betray me.

"It's not a self-portrait," she decided.

"My friend used to draw while I practiced. Sometimes I was the muse," I remembered the hours we spent in this room. Gabriel and Embry would come in while I was practicing. My mother always said I could only leave once my hour was done, so Embry would sing along or tease me while Gabriel would make sketches in a book I gave him one year for Christmas. It wasn't until he gave me this page that I saw most of his sketches were of me.

"I would love to be somebody's muse," she said longingly, bringing her fingers to the lead-covered page.

"It can be intoxicating," I agreed before looking around to make sure no one else was paying attention to our conversation. My mother would immediately know who drew my likeness.

"I'm so glad we'll be sisters soon, and you can teach me all the ways to find a dashing suitor who uses me as his muse," she was smiling to let me know she wouldn't really hold me responsible for her future prospects, but she was also excited for us to be sisters. Which I was under the impression wouldn't happen.

"I'll go check on the food," I decided, getting up and walking out without waiting for a response.

"I thought I had a month?" I asked, barging into my father's study.

"What?" he asked, distracted by a piece of paper he was holding.

"I thought you told Bartholomew you needed time before you could give him your blessing."

"I did," he agreed.

"His sister just told me she can't wait for us to be sisters, and he referred to me as his fiancée," I pointed out.

"You have your month, Annabelle, but it's merely a formality. He knows he'll have my blessing once the month is up, and he knows you'll say yes once he asks. Unless you plan on turning him down, he's only being precocious."

"I didn't think of it like that," I felt like a child reluctant to grow up, but this wasn't about delaying the inevitable. I needed to change it if I ever wanted the chance to be happy.

"He hasn't done anything untoward to you, has he?" he verified.

"No, he's been…a perfect gentleman," I lowered my definition of the word. He was polite and dutiful, but nothing more. I still wasn't sure if he actually liked me.

"Just give him time, my darling. He has a good heart," he assured me.

I nodded, but wasn't comforted in the least. "His father has been commenting on your absence," I told him.

"I'll be out in a minute," he assured me.

CHAPTER 11

The following week, Dr. Smith left suddenly to visit his daughter, leaving Gabriel in charge. He took his responsibilities very seriously, checking on all the patients and making himself available should anyone need him. I was incredibly proud, although I missed seeing him.

"This was his dream," Embry reminded me as he accompanied me in the shops, looking for ribbons.

"He loves helping people," I agreed, smiling at his eternal optimism and belief in the goodness of everyone.

"Reminds me of someone," he teased, showing me a dark red sample.

"That looks like blood," I argued.

"Did you hear about the accident in the forest?"

"What accident?" I asked, not sure if I needed to be concerned yet.

"They were at the lumber yard and little Edwin McAllister came to bring his father some food, but no one saw him, and —"

"Oh, don't tell me," I warned, flinching from the images my mind conjured up.

"He's not dead," he assured me.

"No, but I'm sure he's mangled, and I don't want to hear about it."

"I mean, he'll never be the way he was, but he's a lot better than he could have been. I don't know all the details, not that I would tell them to you if I did, but Gabriel convinced them not to cut off the whole arm, and I'm told he's doing very well."

"Very well considering he only has one arm," I corrected.

"The point is, everyone who has told me the story called Gabriel a hero," he explained why he felt the need to tell me about the horrific accident.

"He is," I agreed, causing Embry to shake his head.

"How's it going with your betrothed?"

"He told you about that?" I asked. I'd made it a point not to mention Bartholomew to anyone, in case they got the wrong impression.

"Maria overheard your mother telling mine," he explained. "I think she fancied him."

"She can have him," I sighed. "His entire family came over the other day, talking like the engagement is secure and the wedding has all but happened," I sighed, trying to focus on the fabric, but my heart was beating fast. Not in the good way it did when Gabriel was close, but in a terrible way where I feared my one chance for happiness was slipping away.

"Have you told your family you don't want to marry him?"

"They know. They're just under the impression I'm reluctant to leave them and grow up or something, not that I'm in love with someone else."

"If they've seen the two of you together, there's no way they don't know."

"We're not that bad," I argued.

"You know, I thought I was in love with you once." He looked up at me with a nervous smile.

"You thought?" I asked.

"Or I was," he amended. "But then I saw the way you looked at Gabriel. I was fine with the way he looked at you, because there's nothing like competition to win a woman's heart, but when I saw you were looking at him the same way, like your heart beat for him alone...I decided I wasn't going to be in love with you anymore."

"How does that work?" I asked, hoping I wouldn't have to do the same.

"Lucky for me I caught it early. And I realized that loving you would break three hearts and destroy any chance of me ever finding happiness, so I had a lot of motivation."

"When was this?" I asked.

"Maybe a month after you arrived in Boston?" he scratched his temple, more to hide the fact that he was blushing than to help him think.

"No one has been in love with me that long," I argued. Not to mention that I had moments up until recently where I was convinced Embry cared for me as more than friends.

"I'm pretty sure you had him under your spell the moment he first saw you."

"That would mean he enjoyed the way I looked, not that he loved me."

"It would. Only the way he explains it, you were there, carrying a doll and a very fat cat, comforting him that this was a nice adventure and the people would be very kind, and you would protect him if they weren't. Promising him that he had nothing to worry about, because you would take care of him."

Gabriel had been alone the first time I met him, standing with his father a few feet away from where I was waiting for my father to ensure all of our belongings would be brought

53

to the plantation for us. I was fairly certain I had moved on to playing with my doll while Maurice chased rats by the time I spotted Gabriel.

"I can't marry Bartholomew," I told him honestly, my heart breaking at the thought of it.

"I know," he said, but there wasn't really much he could do. "If I know Gabriel, I know that he loves you, and there is nothing in the world he wouldn't do to make you happy. He'll win your parents over."

"Or we can run off together."

"The three of us? Or is this a couples thing?" he asked.

"You're always invited Embry. You truly are my best friend." Even now that I wasn't supposed to interact with them, I never found anyone else I could talk to like I did to them. Eugenia was wonderful, and she was my favorite person to talk to at dances and other social functions, but Embry and Gabriel were where I could be myself and come home.

"You're definitely in my top two," he teased before someone pushed through the store's entrance with such speed that we both jumped and turned to look.

"There you are." Gabriel was out of breath, like he'd been running through town searching for us.

I was worried at first, but then I saw his smile.

"What's going on?" I asked as the shop owner lazily swatted at him and returned to the back room.

"Dr. Smith says I am ready to make house calls and treat people without him," he beamed.

"So soon?" I asked, surprised, but relief was already flooding my heart.

"He says he was so impressed with how I handled everything in his absence that, while he would still like to take me with him whenever possible, to give me a more complete education, he feels confident to let me go off and establish my own practice. I already have three families who've requested me, mostly thanks to your father, but..."

"You're like a real physician now," I understood.

"I'll always be learning, but the title is mine to use, and I can start earning an income."

"This is wonderful," I said, taking him in for a hug. I knew it wasn't proper and it lasted longer than it should have, but I felt like I could breathe easy for the first time in forever. Gabriel was now the suitor with prospects that they expected me to marry, so I no longer needed to mislead Bartholomew.

"Congratulations," Embry told the both of us. There was a hint of sadness behind his eyes, but he was genuinely happy for us.

"I came to you as soon as he told me," he explained his state.

"We have to tell my father," I smiled at him, biting down on my bottom lip to prevent myself from kissing him right there in the middle of the shop.

CHAPTER 12

The driver raised an eyebrow, but couldn't really argue with me, especially since we had the open carriage today. The drive to the plantation felt like the longest fifteen minutes of my life, possibly because it was the last fifteen minutes before the rest of my life could begin. We sat apart from each other, and I kept my hands neatly folded in my lap so I wouldn't reach out to grab his.

"You're home early," my mother met me in the foyer. "Did Eugenia not show?"

"She did, but she couldn't stay long. Embry accompanied me until I ran into Mr. Black," I lied, having always intended to see Embry. The words sounded funny, as I only ever used Gabriel's last name to tease him, but I felt the added touch of propriety might please her.

"Mr. Black," my mother's smile dropped when she saw him come in behind me. "How kind of you to accompany Annabelle home."

"It was my pleasure," Gabriel told her.

"Is papa home?" I asked, looking around, wondering if it

was best to ask her to get him, or to walk past her and find him myself.

"I believe he's in his study. What's going on, Annabelle?"

"Gabriel has some very exciting news," I said, suddenly nervous under her apprehensive stare.

She followed us to the study, where my father had left the door open. This was always a good sign.

"Find what you were searching for?" he asked without looking up from his papers.

"I did," I told him, having trouble containing my excitement.

He looked up quickly to smile at my happiness, but did a double take when he saw Gabriel.

"Mr. Black."

"Mr. Owens," Gabriel was nervous, but still smiling.

"How is the apprenticeship going?" my father made conversation.

"Very well sir, thank you. In truth, Dr. Smith recently decided I was ready to set up my own practice. He would still mentor me, of course, but I have already started building up clients, and—"

"And you would like us to pay to have you on call for us," my father finished for him, like he understood exactly what was going on.

"No sir, there is only one thing I want from you, and it isn't money."

"How can I help you, Gabriel?"

"I would like to have your blessing to marry your daughter, if she'll have me." Any bit of the happiness he'd managed to hide thus far resurfaced with a vengeance. "As a physician I will make decent money. I can build a practice and provide her with a home, status, and all the love in the world to ensure she has everything she needs and more. I know I don't deserve her, no one does, but I would like to spend the rest of my life trying to."

Gabriel took my hand in his at the end, and I smiled at him before focusing on my father. I don't know what made me think that he would be happy for me and smiling as well, but he looked...not quite disappointed, but definitely not happy as he sighed, bringing his hands together.

"I'm sorry, but I can't," he apologized.

"You can't?" Gabriel repeated.

"I know you love my daughter and you will be good to her, but I'm afraid you're too late. Another man has already asked for her hand and I have given him my word. It would be my pleasure to support you in your new career, but Annabelle is spoken for."

"You said I had a month," I reminded him.

"Before I gave the blessing, yes, but he knows he has it. The matter has been discussed and although Bartholomew won't ask for another three days, he is under the impression that he is marrying you, and I can't go against that. I'm sorry Gabriel, I truly am."

"You're going to be late," my mother said, just as I was about to argue.

"Right, I must leave, but I can drop you off if you would like."

"Thank you, I appreciate it," Gabriel said, looking entirely defeated.

I looked from one to the other with absolutely no idea what was going on. My father said no, just like that, and Gabriel was accepting it.

"Papa," I tried to stop him, even putting my hand on his arm.

"I'm sorry, my darling, but I have a meeting I simply cannot miss. I'll be home in a few hours."

"But..."

"I'll be back," my father promised before heading out.

CHAPTER 13

"I know this feels like the end of the world, but it isn't. Childhood crushes fade. Bartholomew might not be the most interesting man, but he is kind and caring and he will provide for you. He has a wonderful house that you can turn into a home, a large fortune…you won't want for anything," my mother told me. I just kept staring out the window, at the trees we climbed, the one we carved our names into, all of the dreams I had for my life that would never come true.

"Have I ever told you about Christopher?" she asked, taking my silence as a sign for her to continue. "He grew up n the property beside mine, where his father tended to the ses, and I was so in love with him. I dreamed of marrying nd living happily ever after…"

d then what? You found Papa, someone of your social were much happier?" I asked, hating her more than anyone before. I was convinced I could have her see my side if she hadn't been there. In fact, ven be in this position if she hadn't orches-

"You make it sound so terrible, but I grew up deep in the country. My parents rarely took me into town, and Christopher was the only person my age. He was my best friend and I thought I loved him, but I didn't have a clue what love was, I just knew that I enjoyed spending time with him. When I finally went to town with my mother and met your father, it was like an explosion inside my chest. I never knew that you could care about a person that way, to want to be with them every minute, to miss them the instant they left the room. I could have spent my entire life thinking I was in love with Christopher, only because I didn't know any better, and never gave anyone else a chance," she said.

"I don't love Gabriel because I never gave anyone else a chance," I argued.

"You've known him since the day you arrived, he's comfortable--" she started, but I cut her off.

"No," I disagreed. "I love him because he is where my heart is. When something good happens to me, he is the first person I want to share it with. When I'm afraid, or sad, he is the person I want to turn to. I could give Bartholomew or any other suitor a million chances, but the only person I want to spend the rest of my life with is Gabriel Black. No one will ever love me, or be better for me than Gabriel. He didn't grow up with as much as us, but he has been working every single day, both at the factory and with Dr. Smith, so he can learn the skills and build a practice to take care of me, to be worthy of your blessing." The very thought of it made my blood boil. "I love you mama, but I have waited my whole life for you to accept Gabriel, to see that he is more than good enough. I thought becoming a doctor would be sufficient, but he shouldn't have to do any of it. You should see that he is worthy simply because he loves me. And I love him," I told her.

She had been looking at me with a growing uncertainty, that turned to horror at some point, when she understood the extent of my feelings for Gabriel.

"He isn't your Christopher," she voiced her realization.

"No, he's my everything," I agreed.

CHAPTER 14

My mother left me alone in my father's study, but it wasn't like I could just stand here while my dreams were crumbling around me. I had to get out of here, to do something, anything to try and hold on to them. My father had taken the carriage, so I was forced to take a horse from the stables. My first thought was to find Gabriel, but I doubt he would agree to run away with me if it meant losing my family and destroying my father's honor in the process. I next thought of Aunt Elena, who always managed to know the right thing to say, but I don't think there was anything she could do. I felt like there was a war raging inside my chest, and I either had to let it out or it would drown me, but I feared that if I didn't keep it contained, I could never get it back in.

I thought of Bartholomew and how I could have lived with his lack of a sense of humor, and maybe even been happy, if I had never met Gabriel. Never fallen in love with him. I always thought it would be the idea of breaking Embry's heart that would stop me from acting on my feelings for Gabriel. I never imagined it would be because I was promised to another man.

Without realizing it, I'd ridden to the cottage the Mayweathers were renting. I saw Edith first, picking flowers from the garden, her red hair so much longer than I'd expected. It was beautiful, now that she wasn't hiding it.

"Miss Owens!" she said excitedly when she saw me.

"Is your brother at home?" I asked, getting off the horse and taking a deep breath. I didn't know what I was going to say to him, but I knew that I had to try.

"He's over there with Miss Dante," she said, nodding over to the fields behind her. "We were together making a bouquet, but this is where the yellow flowers are," she explained.

"Maria?" As I said it, I saw them in the distance, not doing anything improper, but she was looking at him the way I knew I looked at Gabriel, and if I wasn't mistaken, he was looking at her in the same way.

"Annabelle," Maria said, shocked when she noticed me.

"Miss Owens," Bartholomew said, taking a step back.

"I came to confide in you, heart to heart, but I feel like you've just shown me yours," I shared. I wondered if every time I thought he was frustrated I was making him wait, he was really upset that I wasn't Maria.

"There is nothing going on, Miss Dante and I were simply walking with Edith when…"

"Of course," I stopped him from whatever lie he was coming up with.

"How can I help you, Miss Owens?" he asked.

"I wasn't sure what I thought would come of this conversation, but now I am hoping we can all find our happiness."

"You have your answer then?"

"To the question I haven't let you ask?"

"Is that not why you are here?"

"I'm here to plead for you to release my father from his word."

He looked at me, shocked, then for a second I saw anger, before he stopped and looked to Maria. "Our families are expecting us to marry, Miss Owens. Anything else would be…"

"Better for the both of us," I said pointedly. "Do you even want to marry me?" I asked, and although I think he might have wanted to at the beginning, I believe he hadn't for a long time.

"My father asked, and I—"

"I made you wait," I tried to remind him how frustrating it had been for him.

"Is this because of Ga-- Mr. Black?" Maria spoke up. She had been silently listening to the man she loved trying – unconvincingly – to get me to marry him.

"I love him with all my heart," I agreed.

Bartholomew looked to Maria, then to me, and said, "My father wants what he wants, Miss Owens. Even if I wanted to…" he let the thought linger.

"Why me?" I asked.

Once more, he looked to Maria, as if her reaction weighed more in his decision to share than mine did. "My father has a business deal that risks to ruin us, but if your father's company shows an alliance to us, no one would dare act on it," he admitted.

His words brought an anger that made me want to slap him. Losing Gabriel to protect an innocent man's heart and my father's reputation was one thing, but losing him to be a pawn in a business transaction that uses my father's reputa-tion…it left an awful taste in my mouth. The only thing that prevented me from following through on the impulse was the fact that Bartholomew looked as disgusted at the prospect as I felt. No wonder he'd been miserable for the past month.

"What if my father agreed to show his support for your family's business regardless?" I suggested.

"Why would he do that?"

"I am hoping my father cares enough about my happiness to not let this ruin four lives," I explained, trying to sound confident. My father had sounded like he wanted to say yes to Gabriel, but it was a question of honor that stopped him.

"If you can convince your father to show his support, I can surely convince my father to release you," he said to me, but his eyes were focused on Maria, with a smile I had never seen on him before.

"Thank you," I told him. For the first time since meeting him, I wanted to kiss him.

I rushed back to my horse, keenly aware of Edith following me, knowing she must have listened to every word. "You're still welcome at the plantation any time you'd like," I told her.

"I hope you mean that!" she called after me as I rode off.

"Absolutely," I yelled behind me.

CHAPTER 15

I rode to my father's office, not sure what I could say to persuade him, but willing to try anything. Unfortunately, he wasn't there, and neither was the carriage. I tried Uncle Robert's, but was told they were out of town, so my father couldn't be with him. I went to every place I could think of, but couldn't find him anywhere.

I eventually went home, figuring I would wait for him and plead my case as soon as he got home. I put the horse in the stables and tried to steady my nerves. I was about to go into the house to get cleaned up when I saw the carriage in the distance. I ran over with my dress hiked up, not even caring that my mother wouldn't approve. It took a moment for the driver to notice me, before he stopped the carriage and my father stepped out.

"Is everything okay?" he asked.

"No," I admitted, trying to wipe away the tears before I gave up and let them fall. "I lied, papa, when I said I would marry Bartholomew, I didn't mean it. Or I did, but I was hoping that you would come around and see how incredible

Gabriel is and give him your blessing instead. That's all I've wanted for as long as I can remember."

"Annabelle—"

"No, you have to listen, papa. I can't marry Mr. Mayweather, and I don't think you want me to. I know you don't want to go back on your word, but I spoke to him, and as long as you don't mind taking his company under your protection, he would be happy to release me and marry someone else. I don't know what the details of his business are, but I know that it would destroy me if I had to be without Gabriel. He is literally the best man I have ever met, and he will love me and be good to me, which I know is what you really want, deep down."

"Is that so?" my father asked while I regained my breath.

"It is," I said, determined.

"I was asking Gabriel," he explained.

I was surprised to see Gabriel climb out of the carriage, followed by my mother. I had thought my father was alone, with my mother still inside the house, wondering where I went.

"Yes, sir. I would give the very heart in my chest if it meant I could spend the rest of my life with her."

"And if she married another?"

"Then I would be her friend, and be there for her if ever she needed anything. Forever." Gabriel didn't say it, but it was clear that although he meant it, his heart would break in the process.

"Okay then," my father sighed.

"Okay then what?" I asked.

"If you love him and believe he will make you happy, then I will speak to Mr. Mayweather. I'm sure we can come to an arrangement."

"You won't give Bartholomew your blessing?" I verified.

"In light of your declaration, your mother's insistence, and Gabriel's eloquent defense, I am giving it to him."

"In that case…"

Gabriel came forward and brought me to the edge of the field, under the oak tree we'd carved our names into. I could feel my parents watching as he went in front of me and got down on one knee, but at least they couldn't hear.

"Bells, you are the love of my life. I knew it the first moment I saw you, and I fall more in love with you every day. My heart can hardly contain how happy you make me just by being near. I know I can't offer you everything you grew up with, but I will spend every day for the rest of my life loving you. Will you do me the honor of being my wife?" Every word was grounded in the certainty of his feelings, but with the weight of his question as well. Like my answer to it was all that mattered.

"Yes," I told him, looking into those deep brown eyes I loved so much. "A million times yes, with all my heart."

He took a ring from his pocket and slipped it on my finger, but I didn't even have time to get a good look at it before he took me in his arms and twirled me. I wrapped my arms around him and he kissed me, like he had done once before, just a few feet from where we were now standing. This time, even though I knew my parents could see, I had absolutely no fear.

The End

***

If you enjoy backstories, make sure to find out how Caleb met Etta in Etta: A Gifted Chronicles Novella…

ABOUT THE AUTHOR

Amanda Lynn Petrin grew up on the South Shore of Montreal with a big and supportive family. She studied Psychology and History at McGill University, then went into acting once she graduated.

In 2017 she moved to Toronto, Ontario, in the hopes of finding more opportunities. Instead, she discovered that you need to create your own. She has written, produced and starred in multiple short films, including Get-Together, All the Things, and Touched. Being an author was a dream she thought would never come true until she started doing the things that scared her. Her debut novel, Shards of Glass, was released in August 2019, and she is just getting started.

Find her at: https://www.amandalynnpetrin.com

ALSO BY AMANDA LYNN PETRIN

Shards of Glass

The Owens Chronicles

Prophecy (Book One)

Destiny (Book Two)

Legacy (Book Three)

The Gifted Chronicles

First Life

Second Chance

Third Eye

www.ingramcontent.com/pod-product-compliance
Lightning Source LLC
Chambersburg PA
CBHW020313150626
46552CB00022B/2873